SAVE THAT TRAIN!

BOOKS FOR BOYS

IAN WHYBROW
ILLUSTRATED BY MARK BEECH

For Teddy Traynor – my favourite grandson.

Text copyright © 2013 Ian Whybrow
Illustrations copyright © 2013 Mark Beech
First published in Great Britain in 2013
by Hodder Children's Books

1

A Catalogue record for this book is available from the British Library

ISBN 978 1 444 91573 0

Printed and bound by CPI Group (UK) Ltd, Croydon, CR0 4YY

The paper and board used in this paperback by
Hodder Children's Books are natural recyclable products made from
wood grown in sustainable forests. The manufacturing processes conform
to the environmental regulations of the country of origin.

Hodder Children's Books
A division of Hachette Children's Books
338 Euston Road, London NW1 3BH
An Hachette UK company
www.hachette.co.uk

The Wormold Family

In the old days, when I was nine or ten, there wasn't a lot of money about, but I was happy enough. I wanted to go off around the world, having adventures, but Dad said, "No, Philip. You need to stay on at school and study." His dream, he was always telling me, was that one day I would be a *somebody*.

Dad was a brilliant carpenter but he never thought he was anybody at all, even though he was so clever with his hands. My mum was house-proud and a smashing cook. Mostly she was sweet-tempered but woe betide you if you did anything to upset the neighbours! Then she would give you a mighty whack with her wooden spoon.

So that was us, the Wormold family. And everyone was pinning their hopes on me to pass my exams and be a bit special. Not that I minded all that much being a nobody. What with my bike and my comics and my marbles and my rabbits, life wasn't too bad.

But there was one thing I really-really wanted. I wished I could be friends with Mickey Durston.

Me, Mickey Durston and Martin

Mickey Durston, he didn't exactly have a gang. I mean, not the sort that goes round picking fights with people, nothing like that. He was just a natural leader, and lads wanted to be in his company.

At school, he was captain of every sport and he was brilliant with a ball. All I knew was that I wished I could be as confident

5

and sure of myself as he was. And if
I couldn't be like him, I wanted to
be in with him.

But me in Mickey Durston's gang?
No way. I wasn't good enough, not
at sport, not at anything, and he didn't
want to be seen around with a weedy
Wormhole.

Never mind, I thought. *I've got
Martin Bale as my best friend.*

Martin was a funny, cheerful long streak of a kid. Mum and Dad liked him: they thought he'd be a good example to me, being a bank manager's son. Martin and I had an understanding about Mickey Durston. "Mickey Durston?" Martin would say, slapping me on the back to show whose side he was on. "I can't *stand* him. He thinks he's IT!"

"Put it there!" I would agree. "He thinks he's IT!" We were real pals and when we were together we had such a lot of fun that time flew by.

The Javver Boys

Who would have thought playing an innocent game like *Javver Boys* would cause so many problems?

Martin and I knew about javelins from school. We had never actually seen a real one, but we enjoyed hurling a broom-handle at a bucket down the end of the garden. Mum wasn't too keen on this because of her chrysanthemums getting flattened, so we invented a game where you had pretend-javelins, invisible ones. They collapsed like telescopes so that you could tuck them into your belt or down your sock. Then you had to crawl about in the undergrowth looking for an enemy or a lion or something. When you saw one, you had to shout "Javver Boys!" then go for your weapon and let fly with it.

Sometimes this would turn into a version of Cops and Robbers. That meant waiting for pretend bank robbers to try making a getaway. We would pop out from round the corner and shout, "Hold it! Hands up! This is the Javver Boys. You're under arrest!" Naturally, the robbers would try to shoot us. Then we would shake out our invisible javelins to their full length, and *Ker-plunk! Aghhhh!* they would find themselves pinned by their sleeves and trouser legs against a door.

Then the bank manager would come out and shake us by the hand. *Well done, Javver Boys! You have earned a huge reward!*

I don't know who had the idea

of bursting the tyres of getaway cars. Could have been either of us.

We were in Station Road, along by the goods yard. We liked to go there sometimes to watch the goods trains through the railings as they puffed along to pick up coal wagons and stuff.

A small green van came chugging along the road, heading for the gates of the yard.

"It's a kidnapper!" I hissed, grabbing Martin by the sleeve. "He's escaping with a film star. He's left a ransom note asking for a million dollars. What are we gonna do about it?"

"I see the swine!" said Martin. "Go for his tyres!"

At once our hands reached down to our socks. *FFFT FFFT!* Two invisible telescopic javelins opened up to their full length. *Shooom!* They flew with deadly accuracy and stopped the kidnapper's van in its tracks.

EEEEEEEK! The real green van swerved and screeched to a halt. Out jumped the driver. "You little devils!" he yelled.

What, us?

"Yes, you! What do you mean by throwing stones at my van?"

Our mouths fell open. Our arms stretched wide. We were innocent. "But we didn't! We …"

"Don't tell lies! Look at this dent you just made in my bonnet! I saw you do it!" Suddenly he turned on his heel. "And you saw them, too, sir, didn't you!"

"I most certainly did, Mr Hedges!" came the thundering reply from a tall man who was marching towards us.

We knew him straight away. The tall man, wonderfully smart from his shiny black boots to his peaked cap, was none other than the fearsome station master! He was important.

13

He was frightening. We didn't hang around to have a chat.

"I know your father!" he roared as we ran. "You're Mr Bale the Bank Manager's son! You'll pay for this, you mark my words!"

Out in the Cold

It was true. The Station Master *did* know Mr Bale. And he did get in touch. He gave a full report to him about how his wicked son and another young criminal were seen hurling stones at an innocent engine driver's van.

The unfairness of it! How *could* those grown-up men both say they'd seen us throwing stones? All right, we *looked* like we were throwing

15

stones and we should never have run away. And then there *was* a dent in the bonnet of the van. So what could we have said to calm those angry voices, those furious red faces?

As I expected, once the station master had complained about us to Mr Bale, Martin was forbidden to come calling for me. When Mum asked me why I was hanging around the house and why she hadn't seen Martin for ages, I told her his family had visitors.

After that, I would set off every morning calling cheerio, and saying I was going round Martin's house. In fact, I was riding my bike – just riding and riding.

One morning, the weather turned chilly. I was banging along on the old bike trying to warm up, but my hands and face were freezing. I turned off the road on to the rough old cinder path that ran along by the railway tracks on the opposite side to Station Road. Through the thick bindweed that swarmed all over the wire fence, I was getting glimpses of the station and the goods yard beyond, with its tall water tower.

I did a flashy dismount, noticing a short Y-shaped stick, good and solid, perfect for a catapult. I bent to pick it up and suddenly I heard strange plinky-plonky music coming from the signal box up by the level crossing.

Bit by bit, the sound became more tuneful, more catchy. I slipped the Y-shaped stick into my back pocket and wheeled my bike to where the music was coming from.

I soon found myself at the bottom of some wooden steps leading up to the signal box. A large notice said:

OFFICIAL RAILWAY PERSONNEL ONLY

I knew I shouldn't, but I climbed those steps and pressed my nose against the smeary glass of the panelled door at the top.

Over in a corner of the signal box, the coals in the belly of a little black stove glowed and flickered warm red and orange. On top of the stove was one of the signal-man's booted feet.

Suddenly the *plinka-plonka* stopped. The man must have noticed me because he let out a yell.

Oh, no! I was in trouble again! I turned and dashed down the steps as fast as my legs would carry me.

The Signal Box

I hadn't got to the bottom of the steps before I heard the door being whipped open behind me. "You're all right, son!" came a friendly voice.

I turned and found myself looking up into the smiling, whiskery face of Mr Walker! I knew him – by sight, anyway. He lived in one of the old cottages down Gaol Lane, not far from our house. I sometimes gave him a wave as he walked by in the early mornings, but I never realized he worked for the railways.

"I-I heard you playing music …" I stammered, pointing to the old banjo that he was holding by the neck. "I thought it was good."

"Really? I was only passin' the time, like," he said, looking pleased. Then he waved his free hand towards the warm. "Come on up if you want."

"Am I allowed?" I said as I stepped in.

"I can't see nothin' wrong with it," he smiled. "There won't be nothin' happenin' for ..." He flipped the pocket-watch out of his waistcoat. "Forty-three minutes," he decided. "Then I shall have to close the crossin' and set the points for the up-train. The station master will be doing his books at the minute, so he won't trouble us."

He must have noticed the blood drain from my face at the mention of the station master. "Ah! You've come across him, have you? Best you keep your head down if he steps out on the platform, look!"

I turned to where he was pointing. The station platform was near enough for me to be able to see that it was deserted except for a porter having a sweep-up.

"The station master keeps a pair of binoculars in his office so he can see what I'm up to," went on Mr Walker. "Don't you fret, though! He hardly ever bothers to come here to pay me a visit. Nobody does."

I could breathe again.

He carefully laid down the banjo. "Cuppa char, son?" he said, grabbing two tin mugs and clinking them together. I said I'd love a cup of tea.

It was nice in the closed world of that warm box, with someone I could talk to. As we sipped our sweet tea with evaporated milk, Mr Walker told me about some of his duties. He had to black the iron frame that held the row of levers, and make entries in his Registration Book

every time a train passed. Then he
pointed out the wheel that closed
the level crossing gates. Some of the
levers were for raising and lowering
signals. Other ones controlled the
points to direct the goods trains
from the sideline of the goods yard
on to the main track.

He stirred and rattled the fire in stove with a poker. "Nearly out of coal," he said. "I shall have to get one of the goods drivers to drop me some off."

"Do you know all the drivers round here?" I asked. "Do you know Mr Hedges?"

"Bill Hedges? Yep! Good old boy he is usually, but he's been like a bear with a sore head lately! One of his teeth has gone rotten and he won't see no dentist to get it fixed."

Mr Walker was so open and friendly, I suddenly found myself telling him my troubles. I told him about the Javver Boys and

Mr Hedges' van and how I'd lost my best friend.

Suddenly a buzzer went off and frightened the daylights out of me.

"Ten-minute warning," explained Mr Walker. He looked at me thoughtfully. He knew what it was like to be lonely. "I tell you what, boy, I got to start concentratin', like, so you better toddle off now. But look, you can come up here and have a chat any time you feel like it, if I ain't busy."

I thanked him and got up to face the chilly morning.

"Here, you'll be needin' this," he said, handing over a good stout length of elastic. "Only watch where you're shootin', eh?"

He'd noticed the Y-shaped bit of wood sticking out of my back pocket. "By the way," he went on, "if you ain't got nothin' special to do, you might take a message down to the old brewery. A little bird told me there's a bunch of kids makin' themselves a den in an old box-car parked on the sidings there. You know the place I mean, close by the entrance to the tunnel what runs under Lee Hill? Now the thing is, my little bird tells me that the station master is plannin' to make a surprise visit to inspect the sidings. Maybe not today or tomorrow – but soon. So why don't you tell them to hop it before they get into serious trouble."

I thanked him, and pretended that I would ride over there straight away. But as I bumped and clattered along the rutted cinder path, I was already thinking about heading for home. I didn't want to risk going over to the old brewery. There was only one boy in our neighbourhood bold enough to do something like setting up a den in an old railway carriage. His name was … you guessed it … Mickey Durston.

And who was the *last* person Mickey Durston would take any notice of?

Me.

Chewy Heaven

I must have been looking pretty miserable at teatime because afterwards Dad told me to go and have a look in his jacket that was hanging on the hook by the back door. "I've got something in there that might cheer you up!" he said.

Blimey, I thought all my Christmases had suddenly turned up at once! Dad had brought me home something from the American

 air base where
he worked,
something
that most
English
kids had
never *seen*, let
alone tasted: real American chewing
gum... in *strips*! Suddenly I, Philip
Wormold, was the proud owner of
some chewy that was the stuff of
dreams. Tooti-Frooti flavour gum!
Liquorice flavour gum! Raspberry
flavour gum ... and best of all,
Hubba Bubba *Bubble* Gum!

"Cor! Thanks, Dad!" I said. "This
is my best present EVER!"

After breakfast next day, I
dashed upstairs to collect my gum,

then I jumped on my bike and headed for the churchyard at St Saviours, my jaw champing like a horse at a haybag.

I had just worked out a master plan.

The churchyard was a quiet and under the almond tree round the back there were almonds everywhere, still wrapped in their silky green-grey cases. I filled all my pockets with them – all except my shirt pocket that contained two strips of Hubba Bubba Bubble Gum.

This was the plan. I would ride over and warn

Mickey about the station master coming. He wouldn't believe me at first. He'd think I was just a weedy kid come to try to get in with him. But then he'd notice that I was chewing something.

He'd say, "Hey, what's that in your gob, Weedy?"

 I wouldn't say anything. I would just spit out the licorice gum I was chewing and reach for one of the strips of Hubba Bubba Bubble Gum. I would look him in the eye and just casually carry on chewing. Then I would blow this pink

bubble, a big one. His mouth would fall open. I'd pop the bubble. Then he would beg me. "Hey! Where did you get that? Give us a bit. Go on. Pleeese!"

Then I'd take my catapult out of my back pocket and I'd say, "See that tin right over there on that wall?"

He would say, "Yeah, so what?"

I would say, "Watch."

I'd load the catapult. *TWANG!* ... *CRASH!* That tin would go flying and I would just get on my bike and say, "See ya, Mick."

Then he would shout, "Wait. Don't go! Honestly, Philip, I didn't realize you were a crack shot! Why don't you stay and join my gang?"

"This place isn't safe, Mickey," I'd
say. "But you can come round my
house if you like."

"Great idea, Phil," he'd say.
"You're a pal!"

That was the plan. What could
go wrong?

I took out the catapult, fitted an
almond into the pouch, aimed at
the church notice board,
pulled back the elastic
and let fly.

OWWWWW! The elastic smacked into the side of my wrist. I dropped the blasted catapult and danced round, shaking my throbbing hand.

"Blimey!" I thought. "Let's hope I can do better than that."

Nasty Shocks

Even after I'd practised firing almonds all morning, things didn't quite go to plan.

For a start, I had a heck of a job getting over the old brewery gates. They were really high, with a line of spikes on top. I thought, *Well, Mickey Durston must have climbed them ...* So I gritted my teeth and scrambled over somehow, only I caught my jacket and managed to rip it right up the side.

It was a spooky old place with most of the windows smashed in and weeds growing out of the brickwork. I worked my way over piles of rubble till I came to an overgrown railway track.

Now it was plain to see the railway siding with a box van parked on it, the one that Mr Walker had told me about. It was sitting just off the main line. Not far away was the entrance to the tunnel that cut through Lee Hill.

There was no sign of life except for a flock of sheep in the field that went up steeply on the other side. It was so quiet that I could hear them tearing at the grass. Some of them pressed their heads through the

fence and tugged at the stuff
growing close to the railway track.
There was no sign of any kids at all.
Suddenly I could hear a muffled roar
coming from the tunnel. A few
seconds later, in a choking burst of
smoke, sparks flying, wheels grinding,
out roared a little old steam engine
hauling three coke wagons. And
before I could duck out of sight,
there was Mr Bridges leaning out of
his cab. He had his spotted
neckerchief tied round his jaw, but
that didn't stop him
yelling something at
me and shaking his
fist!

The train chuffed on round the corner in the direction of the station and left me trembling in the silence.

Without warning, there was a shocking rumble from the box car behind me that made me jump like a rabbit. The door slid wide open and out jumped a small, neat boy.

"Wormhole!" he shrilled. It was Graham Cook, one of Mickey Durston's favourites. "You let that driver see you!"

"I didn't do it on purpose," I

protested loudly.

Graham Cook jumped down, took off his jacket and put up his fists. "We saw you. You just stood there and gave yourself away. Come on, Wormhole, put your fists up, you've asked for it."

He was like a little terrier. He was always getting into fights in the school playground and although he was small, he was deadly. He would do hard rabbit punches and deadlegs with his knees.

"I'm not fighting," I said. "I've come to see Mickey."

Graham Cook started singing "Cowardy cowardy custard, Wormhole's in the mustard!"

He kept it up until Mickey

Durston's voice cut him off. "What about?" he demanded. "I've come to warn you," I said. "You've torn your jacket," said Mickey, ignoring me and effortlessly slipping down from the boxcar.

"I did it on the gate," I said proudly.

"That was stupid," said Mickey coldly. "Why didn't you use some common sense and come along the track by the railway? That way, you don't have to climb at all."

I tried to regain some pride. "The station master's after you. And he's bringing a copper."

"So what?" said Mickey. "This is brewery land. It's got nothing to do with the railway. The station master can't touch us and nor can the police."

I never knew a kid as cool-headed as Mickey Durston. Nothing could shake him.

"So ha ha!" scoffed Graham Cook.

That annoyed me. "So how come you were so worried about that driver seeing me, Mister Clever?" I snapped at him.

Graham Cook took a run at me. "Leave him, Cookie!" ordered Mickey.

"The fact is, that engine driver has a violent temper. He'll give you a thump round the ear as soon as look at you."

There was no way he was going to let me stay now … unless … I tapped my shirt pocket. "By the way, I've got some bubble gum," I said as casually as I could. "Hubba Bubba. My dad can get it from the air base any time."

Magic words. I had their attention at last.

Graham Cook was the first to break. He started begging me for bit of chewy. At once, Mickey reached across and gagged his mouth with his hand. He looked at me with those green eyes, only not down his nose for a change. "Fancy a look in my den?" he asked. "I've got someone I'd like you to meet."

It was nice inside, dark with a couple of apple boxes to sit on.

There was only one thing wrong. Sitting in the corner, fiddling with a loose end on his pullover, looking very ashamed of himself … was Martin Bale.

The traitor.

Panic Stations!

I hardly slept a wink that night, I was so angry. Come the morning, I had reached the biggest decision of my life. I would go and tell that high-and-mighty Mickey Durston and his new pal Martin Bale that they could take a running jump.

I was on the bike in two shakes after breakfast, and pedalling like a windmill towards the old brewery.

Even before I got to the brewery

siding, I could hear a terrible noise.
I let the bike drop to the ground,
and ran to where Mickey, Cookie
and Martin were racing up and
down by the fence at the edge of
the railway line. They were waving
their arms and screaming at the tops
of their voices. The sheep had
broken through the fence on the
other side of the railway and
slipped down the steep grassy
embankment on to the line.

There must have been a hundred
of them milling round on the tracks
in front of the entrance to Lee Hill
tunnel. At least one had been killed
by the fall.

"Get back! Go back!" screamed
the boys.

The sheep took not a blind bit of notice.

"What are we going to do?" I yelled to Mickey. "There could be a train coming at any minute!"

"There's nothing we *can* do!" he yelled back. "And the station master and that engine-driver already think we're vandals. They're bound to think we turned the sheep loose!" He barked an order to Cookie and

Martin. "Let's get out of here."

With that, he turned and ran away, with Cookie close behind.

Martin stood his ground. "It's not right," he said. "I'm going down on to the track to flag down any train that comes. It'll be murder if they don't stop in time."

"Don't! You'll get yourself killed!" He took no notice, so I ran and picked up my fallen bike.

"Where are you going?" he shouted.

I was in too much of a hurry to shout anything back. And the last word he shouted went through me like a javelin.

"*COWAAAAARD!*"

Crash!

My legs ached, my knees were bleeding from the time I hit a rut and got thrown over the handlebars, I'd grazed my forehead, but it didn't stop me.

It took all my strength to turn those pedals and I could feel myself losing speed. Any minute now, the up-train might come steaming along!

It seemed to take forever to get to the cinder path and when I did, the back tyre burst with a crack like a firework. But there was nothing for it but to push on. Even with that racket, I could hear the sound I dreaded. It was the warning bell for the level crossing. Mr Walker was closing the gates to stop the cars and let a train through!

I could see smoke begin to rise in clouds. The goods train was crossing the points on to the main line.

Slowly the smoke clouds rose at first – *WUFFF-Wuff-wuff-wuff!*

WUFFF-wuff-wuff-wuff!

I started to pray. "Please God let me get to the signal box before that goods train! And let Mr Walker show him the danger signal!"

I hit a brick and down I went. I struggled to my feet and tried to run, but my legs wouldn't work properly and I collapsed on to my knees. "Mr Walker!" I gasped, waving my arms above my head.

My cries were lost in the gathering noise of the goods train. By the time I began to drag

52

myself towards the signal box, that familiar black F2 engine with a train of coal-trucks in tow was chuffing and creaking and screeching its way over the crossing. As the train drew level with him, Mr Walker gave the driver a wave. The red-spotted neckerchief told me that it was Mr Hedges. He opened the regulator to get up more speed.

The engine came past me at a fast walking pace, though she was getting up steam. It was the fireman who noticed my antics. He pulled Mr Hedges by the sleeve. Together, he and the big-jawed old driver leant out of the cab and hurled insults at me. Suddenly Mr Hedges clutched his jaw. His rotten tooth

must have given him
a twinge.

"Danger ahead!
Sheep on the line!" I
yelled. Neither of
them could hear me,
even that close. On steamed the
goods train, past me, faster and
faster ... heading up the line for the
Lee Hill tunnel.

I glanced at my feet. There on
the path lay my catapult where it
had fallen from my pocket. The
engine was picking up speed. I
snatched up the catapult and
staggered after the train, feeling in
my pockets as I went. *Got one!* My
searching fingers closed round an
almond. I thumbed it into the

leather pouch and stood still. Feet slightly apart, I drew back the elastic as far as I could – and let fly.

SNAP! The pale-green missile sailed in a slight curve towards the cab. On and on it flew. By instinct, the fireman jerked back his head to try to dodge it. I didn't know whether the almond hit him or not. Anyway, the back of his head smacked Mr Hedges in the face – *CRASH!* Up went the driver's hand to his mouth, and when he took it away, it was red with blood.

I thought, "What have I done?" and what happened after that, I'm not too sure. I sat down, or fell down. Mr Hedges must have hit the emergency brake. Then he and the fireman came scrambling up the bank and tried to burst through the fence and give me a hiding.

It was Mr Walker who saved me. "Give the kid a chance to explain!" he bawled at them.

The End of Weedy Wormhole

"Maybe you could be a dentist
when you grow up," said Martin. He
blew a big Hubba Bubba bubble
and snapped it expertly back.
"You're good at taking teeth out."

"Ha ha, very funny," I said, and
blew a bubble of my own.

"Great, isn't it!" he laughed. He
spread his arms and gazed around
at the box car. "All ours!"

It wasn't just great, it was *WHIZZO!*

57

Talk about snug! Nice little table, couple of comfy chairs, carpet, store cupboard – even a couple of lamps. All railway property it was – on loan to us for as long as we wanted!

The furniture was the station master's idea. As he said to our mums and dads on the day they wrote about Martin and me in the newspapers, "It's the least the railway can do after what your boys did. We had all that old furniture in store, so it's nice to find someone to make good use of it. And since the brewery people have no plans to work on that site, they see no harm in letting the boys make use of their box-car for as long as they wish."

Me and Martin – heroes! We had a list as long as your arm of kids wanting to join our gang.

"Cheers, mate," I said, and raised my tin cup to Martin. "Cheers, mate," said Martin and we drank each other's health in fizzy cream soda. There was a whole boxful of it in the corner – a present from Mr Hedges.

If he hadn't listened when he discovered the dent on the bonnet of his van, at least he took notice when Mr Walker had told him to hear me out. Then I'd quickly explained. So when he set off up the line with a gang of men to round up the sheep, he let me ride in his cab. When we reached the scene, we found Martin, still standing firm on the track, waving his pullover like a warning flag.

"Sorry I got you all wrong," Mr Hedges had muttered. "I thought you two were a couple of them *juvenile delinquents* everybody's talking about."

He just kept telling Mum and Dad how lucky they were to have a son who was prepared to risk getting into trouble to help others.

Even Mr Bale patted me on the back. "Jolly good show!" he said. "By Jove, that was quick thinking, laddy! You amaze me! "

I couldn't stop grinning. That was the end of Weedy Wormhole. I half-knew it as soon as I made up my mind to tell Mickey to take a running jump. But when I saw my

name **Philip Wormold** on the front page of the newspaper, I knew it for certain.

"Good," I said to myself. "Good. Now I know what it feels like to be a Somebody."

MAMMOTH ACADEMY

Join friends Oscar and Arabella at the Mammoth Academy!

Neal Layton

Winner of the Smarties Prize

'Overflowing with humour.'
Junior Magazine

www.neallayton.com
www.hodderchildrens.co.uk